SLEEPWALKING

Poems by
NEELASHI SHUKLA

AMARYLLIS

AMARYLLIS

This edition first published in 2013

AMARYLLIS

An imprint of Manjul Publishing House Pvt. Ltd.

7/32, Ground Floor, Ansari Road, Daryaganj,
New Delhi 110 002

Email: amaryllis@amaryllis.co.in

Website: www.amaryllis.co.in

Registered Office:
10, Nishat Colony, Bhopal 462 003, M.P., India

ISBN: 978-93-81506-32-5

Designed by: aquariusppl.com

Printed and Bound in India by:
Thomson Press (India) Ltd.

I wish to thank everyone who took the time to read my poetry and appreciate it; Sylvia Plath, for hypnotizing me by her imagery and metaphors, Agatha Christie for making me relish the obscure, and especially my Mom, because her smile is the best thing that has happened to this world.

CONTENTS

1 Run

In the early light,
I write to you.
Sister, run away.
Who cares about the colours of the right?
When everything else is painted blue,
When the evening is the brightest part of the day.

Violet drops in a vial of death,
Might enter your nostrils,
So, bite your tongue,
And forget literature and Macbeth,
All wild flowers and tendrils,
And run sister run.

In the flickering candlelight,
We learnt to read together,
And then in a wave of a rippling yellow fireball,
Everything was wiped out of sight;
They were burning homes and heather,
And we were losing it all.

A story of a home,
Is entwined within four walls.
Why would a stranger want to conspire with them,

And build up a catacomb,
And grin as the brick falls,
And change the lyrics of our anthem?

They don't care what you do,
Sister, they don't even wait for the sun to lie down,
There is smoke in the air,
Smoke in the view,
Tainted by a vague September brown,
Now, everything has colour there.

We picked up some flowers of peace,
And rode on stigmas,
And we were exiled.
And now, bit by bit, piece by piece,
We try to recollect the traumas,
And reason why, we still smiled.

Some fanatics,
Treaded on simmering 'noons,
Barefoot on a humid truce,
And they counted the fallen bricks,
And stones and sand dunes,
And they attacked with their shoes

There were drops of a rainfall hope,
When he was handed over the crown,
But our souls are chained,
And our hearts strive to elope;
And although he was brown,
It never really rained.

The man on the throne,
Pretends to help us,
And as I scribble,
My hands drone,
The sun collides with the focus,
And with colours, I see him dribble.

He pretends to help us,
But it's past midnight.
So Sister, whisper a rushed goodbye,
And catch the airbus,
That leads you to a southern height,
In the flocculating light of a transparent sky.

When colours are dyeing to dictate,
And our voices are at the aphelia,
Take your daughter, take your son-
The dawn might be late,
When the dusk is the paraphernalia,
-And run, Sister, run.

And waiting for a lilac sun,
And wishing that the knots were undone,
And witnessing a bombarded fragment,
Of sandstone and cement,
You will realize,
That you have lost your eyes.
The night has gulped down,
With a shade of a slanderous brown,
With a draught struck thirst,
And an abrupt outburst,
With non crying eyes,
Of a ruined sunrise,
Mesopotamia. ■

2 Before Birth

What came of you River?
Did someone strip in front of you,
Jump into you,
And swim from this world to yours?
Did someone dissolve in you?
Was that someone ash-like; powdery?
Or supple sore-like; bleeding?
Or solid stone-like; hurting?
Did you silently watch?
Or did you roar and leap and cuddle them with pity?
Or was that your love for blending nature with its babies?
Or were you angry at such limpid acts of shame?
Were you proud they were joining your parade?
Or were you plain stark white mean?
Laughing and flapping your gooey wings?
Sardonic, was it?
Were you standing flat-
Plastering your knees to sludge-
And, pathetically lonely?
Were you just a bystander?
The one that walks by Gandhi,
He hasn't seen darkness,

He hasn't heard a whimper,
He hasn't spoken against blackness,
He has lived in whiteness,
Plainness,
He has lived smiling.
He rides a bicycle and he swishes,
He sees and he passes,
Though it pokes him from time to time,
He dissolves it in your magnanimous folds,
And one day,
when dormancy devours all the remaining parts of him,
He finally decides,
To take that jump,
And then you stand there,
Emulating him, perhaps,
Or is it the galvanized you?
Transcended, adapted to newer hues,
And you don't as much as ripple,
When that jump
Occurs,
Slow motioned,
A timeless semantic of
An eternal coupling;
The debts of life,
The calm of your skin,
The fabric of passiveness. ■

3 Afternoons

The biscuit sun exists.
I have seen it.
My son has chewed bits of it.
It's so soft and humble.
It melts in the mouth.
But I see no sugar around.
Maybe his tongue plays tricks.
Or maybe he has learnt that gimmick from the black clown we had.
By the way he was our cook.
He made sumptuous turkey.
I am not like the other Feudal women.
I let him eat in the kitchen after dark.
Tim liked him.
By the way, Tim is my son.
I went for Motion Pictures.
They were also called black and white.
I am not a blonde.
The Brunette in me thinks that they are not black and white.
They are black and grey.
Tim is four years old.
He has a bike.
Jim makes him ride it.
What a delight to watch him saddle his horse.

Thank God, he's a boy.
Samantha said, Jim is a boy too.
I say shut up.
He is our cook.
Then I remember my Nanny.
She told me the sun was orange.
But when I grew older, I discovered it was yellow.
Then one day I asked her
Why she lied to me.
She said she didn't.
It was orange and even red in the part she came from.
Then I told my teacher.
She spanked me.
Nanny was black.
I was baking cookies once.
They came out hard.
I refused to eat them.
Tim puked after he did.
I did the sensible thing after that.
I gave them to Jim.
My neighbour's wife calls me so generous.
She says she keeps a bamboo stick with her.
You never know with servants.
Time runs so fast.
I was watching this song on Mtv.
I am 50 now.

A black boy surrounded by black and white skimpy girls.
He's topping the billboard.
But what a pity.
He doesn't sing at all.
He just mutters breathlessly.
'Rhythm and Poetry' I can write much better.
Then there is this girl.
Making songs on an umbrella.
But c'mon
The flat noses can't be pretty.
What has the world come to?
I look out of my window.
It's not summer anymore.
The sun is like the moon.
Both pale, mellow.
It loses its luster.
But I still find the luster in my past-
When I recount Tim riding his bike.
But Tim never cared for a sunbath.
Or anything else.
He's married a Blonde now.
It's lucky to be the only Brunette in the family.
And then the sun sets.
When I sleep,
I dream of it.
It doesn't even come out orange.
It's biscuit.

And Tim relishes it.
Then Tim's face blurs.
I don't see him at all.
Instead,
I get all my luster back.
I discover the biscuit sun exists.
And it's prettier than anything I have ever seen.
It's been a long time.
I see a man standing with open arms.
After all that has happened in the past.
He's not violent.
He's not grey and black.
He is full of sparkle.
He lives where the biscuit sun exits.
And I smile in my sleep.
The man is Jim. ■

4 Corners, Corners

Toddlers play such games.
From one corner to another corner,
Of walls and pretty walls;
Pink walls and cherry walls.
Wall to wall,
Holding hands,
Losing grip,
Moving here,
Sliding there,
Blindfolded,
And looking at the wonder of what has been made,
Of walls.
Toddlers,
Play such games.

Holding your heart.
And fondling your ruffled hair,
There is a spoilt son in every man,
A geek: in every daughter.
Who, doesn't know how to love,
Who, wants to be accepted,
Beyond that hot pink wall,
Towards a black gothic wall,
But don't toddlers,
Play such games??

A basket of fish,
Stinks in your hand.
There is a sea in every son,
A butcher: in every mother.
The sea reeking of a fishy existence,
And the butcher,
Feeding his ego,
With every fish that he owns,
And sells.

It's too late to be thinking about you,
It's dark enough to be thought about.
There is a bat in every woman,
Blind in the night,
Snoring in the day,
And there is an owl in every man,
Beyond suits and ties,
And orderly walls,
Hooting in the night,
Alert of the existence of one such bat,
Who, wants to be 'Batman'.
And then, the night is a wall,
And dawn another wall,
And fidgeting between transitions,
Both jump from wall to wall.
Toddlers,
Play such games.

Thunders,

And motorcycles, of little things.
There is a rustic in sophistication,
That makes sophistication, sophistication.
Adventure percolates down to housewives,
And doormats.
Another stormy affair,
In the tides of men,
Seeping through a social wall,
And a dominated red wall,
Women transcend from corners to,
Other corners,
In corners,
Of masculine walls.
But, don't toddlers,
Play such games?

Nail polish,
Pink acetone-less,
Avaricious handbags,
And credits.
There is a teenage girl in every man,
Because attraction is another name,
Given to self-love.
And mirror, mirror,
On the wall,
Who is the villain of them all?
Snow white on the black wall,
Or Step Mom on the white wall?

Or the Prince?
Who is a pretty prop,
In a female world of fairytale walls?
But,
Toddlers play such games.

And so,
Ring o' ring o' roses,
And there goes a childish drifter,
In eyes of the sun,
And dreams of the moonlight,
Tree houses,
And kittens and stone fruits,
The dream between corners,
Of walls,
And from one wall to another wall,
Another dream calls,
And another toddler jumps,
And another toddler falls,
A toddler laughs,
Another sobs,
Both get up,
To play the same game again.
Yes, toddlers,
Play such games.

5 Beneath the Outlines of Water

In a fish market.
I step on flesh,
Geese and buckets of tomato,
Cherry,
Apple, and bell pepper red,
Blood.
Naphthalene balls,
Swallowed.
Gulped down,
With acid,
Phenyl,
Or the butcher's knife,
The woodcutter's axe maybe…
You dissected my mind,
Into cabaret pieces-
A hideous,
Finless fish-
With a sword within the scales,
-Hung,
In the pungent,
Dark,
Fish market.
A hat soiled in fish eggs,
Piscean prophesies,
And more disgust,
Oozing baskets of rust,
A bid for every lust,
I smile,
You smile.
We are stones. ■

6 Dichotomy

We have crossed paths in another life.
You were my enemy back then.
I slept with you once in broad daylight.
There was a busy street outside bustling with soldier steps,
Sirens, searches, confiscation, exclamation marks.
Some women were wailing,
Some children were strewn on the barracks,
Blue eyes were twinkling all over our town,
Noises and screams were taking turns; oscillating.
I remember your nervous laughter and paranoid smile when I touched you,
You said you might have heard your mother cry out on the street,
But I pretended not to be listening.
As my fingers doughed your creamy skin,
Soldiers plastered yellow stars on people on the streets,
Some were fed with breads baked of blood,
As some old men fiddled amongst corpses for signs of blue,
Their parched throats more brunette than ever,
The only blue they found was in the eyes
Of those men sieving men.
I had the same eyes as these proud men with weapons,
And a thirst that echoed the thirst of those old men.
So I desperately looked for something blue,
Something sacred in you.

I had really liked to help you then.
But you kept looking outside, distracted, uninterested,
Insulting the little remains of mercy left in me,
I had really wanted to help you.
But you didn't have anything blue on you.
I remember your dress was olive that day.
And so, bending my head
In front of the twinkle that had kissed the streets of my town,
I had given you up to bluer men.
Your dress always remained olive after that.
In this life,
You have come to me
With tempt that echoes from that world,
And contempt that shadows my life today,
I still cannot help you out.
I can get swayed in your lure,
But however much it may glitter,
It is still tarnished.
Tarnished,
Not by that olive dress you wore
Or the past that I still recall,
It is tarnished,
For I still cannot help you.
I shall never be able to shirk off those cobwebs that I've some to inherit and abide by,
However drunk, melted and poisoned I might be around you,
The face of Judas shall always haunt me.

7 Missing

1. I couldn't remember anything else,
Music, no music,
A light of blood,
Three kites of blood.
It's been ten years,
Or maybe more,
Since I left you.

Boats of tricks,
Parabolic wood,
Wooden waters,
It's been heaven,
Or maybe more,
But I left you.

Saffron rice,
Blush rose babies,
Green fields,
White idiots,
Three kites of blood,
Rites of blood,
It's been Kashmir,
Or maybe more,
I couldn't remember a thing,
Since the ten years,
That I left you.

2. It was in Nuremberg
Or somewhere just as bad,
That I lost you.
Fluid, sleeping in Hitler's hands,
I lost you.
To a war,
A trial,
Kids, cyanide,
Gunpowder.
Catapulted, captured,
Lost, suicidal,
Suicidal, lost,
Captured,
Catapulted,
Gunpowder,
Gunpowder,
Gunpowder-
Fluid, sleeping, in Hitler's arms,
It was in our marriage,
Or in Nuremberg,
Or something just as bad,
That I,
Lost you.

3. Injuries.
Band-Aid of fifty candles,
Crimson darkness.
A bitter birthday cake.
I missed you.

A road of cardamom,
Green layers.
Black seeds.
Stampede.
Rushing doors.
Coffers.
Coffins.
I missed you.

Eyesight,
No eyesight,
Spectacles of fog,
Lake water cataract,
Flashes of love,
Buckets of age,
Drowned you,
Drowned us.
I missed you.

4. I am angry
For you died.
Ferns grew up.
Etching forest green mountains.
Jade lips.
Lime eyes.
Dirty ferns,
Grew up.
Never stopped,
Blood gushing people,
Ferns,
Lichens, ameba, curdled,
Waited, paused,
Breathed, snored,
Roared, loathed,
Curious, they grew up.
And the ferns,
Far too green ferns,
Grew up.
I am still,
Counting-
Angry. ■

8 Conjunction

When I come to the house
You cry every night.
I know it was awe
And a bagful of dumbness
That made you live with me.
You did not think
I shall cage you like that-
Use you like this
Bend you like that.
Scrape you like this
Peel you like that.
Hate you like this
Feel you like that.
Kiss you like this
Numb you like that.

A kiss of spite,
In a mouthful of apathy,
I swallow your pride,
While you swallow your pride,
Numbing a little more,
Tending to bluer shores.

I gave you plastic cushions from time to time,
My people wore you up their sleeves,
She had you up her head,
You were brimming and it was protocol
I had to take you home.
It rained sometimes,
But you were already so wet,
I had another home
And you were not part of it
Sometimes I wondered how you smelt like basil,
I had to take away your smell,
And carry it home,
Sometimes you made a face,
But it was usually too dark for me to see anything.

You wanted to make your own salt,
I wanted to rape yours,
Your eyes danced with shame,
Mine shone too much in yours,
Yours tried to move away,
Mine pressed too hard,
And you deferred yours to another day.

It took you another man,
Lots of shades of white,
And a bucket full of idealism,
To utter your first words.

This white was unlike mine,
This man was older,
His eyes calm and his fingers on a wheel instead of you.

I could see myself in him,
Maybe that's why I hated him.
Maybe I hated him because he didn't even touch you
And I somewhere wanted him to want you;
Only I didn't realize,
You had always been his.

I couldn't give up this house
And the thought of you and him revolted me,
Repulsion boiled down my throat
And I kissed you again.

Like a dog becomes loyal to a master,
A slave to his owner,
I had not bought you,
But I had touched you enough,
I hated you and somewhere you admired me for it,
I left your doorstep
But I had cut you into half.
I hear the man had frowned,
You had lost a lot of blood
Experienced brain damages,
Several miscarriages,

Buried and burnt nameless sons and daughters,
The old man had succumbed to his own goodness,
My whiteness weaned and re emerged,
Sixty years later
It had changed colours,
Not sides
You had shown brilliance in phases,
You had become like me,
Touching,
Using,
Lusting for a frantic nascent drop
In an ocean of stones,
Frozen,
And tearless,
While the other part of you,
Decays. ■

9 I Slept With A Black Woman

I was in the midst of cardamoms,
I was inhaling brown cocoa caffeine,
I was wandering in green banana plantations,
Sprinkled by a shady Caribbean sun,
And it is funny how the sun can be known by a place or colour,
When there is just one…
And although I say this,
I was black enough,
To sleep with a black woman.

I was in the midst of chlorine bamboos,
Dangling on red soils,
I was with gypsy folks piercing their coloured noses,
And I was amid savannah;
My soul soaking somewhere in those brown mud paddy fields,
And though my colleagues called it vivid,
I thought it was all- dark.
Somehow, my thought painted me,
As I was black enough,
To sleep with a black woman…

I was in the midst of tall mustard grasses,
That were imperial,
For they mellowed and hid beneath their porcupine-like might,

The creatures who,
Inhabited the dusty jungle.
There played ant-tinted kids,
To whom concrete schools weren't novel,
Only enrolment was,
To whom a language called English was not exotic,
Union Jack's Blue Freedom was.
I was in between symbols,
That were silver,
And although it was silver,
It had corroded my smile,
I saw it black,
And turned black enough,
To sleep with a black woman.

I was in the midst of a tribal anticipation;
Crude was an eyesore there.
Here, it became eye candy.
The only difference was,
That the candy was chestnut and bitter chocolate like,
And though I love chocolates,
My relish was dimmed by the frugal third world spirit,
And as I took a reluctant bite,
I realized,
I was becoming black enough,
To sleep with a black woman...

I was in the midst of mucky hutments of the largest continent,
And I thought it disembarked my pride.
So I had nothing to do,

But to stoop down lower,
Talk and eat black and white beneath a clear blue African sky,
Between remnants of diamond and gold mines,
Between erstwhile slaves,
Who were threats,
Between ogling middle class men of my race,
Who looked at the model like girls on the pavements,
That spoke of broken insipid promises.
And I hate them all,
They compromise below a wild cocoon beauty to be occupied,
And I hate to lose my pink-cheeked vanity,
And I hate to face up to the red fact,
That I was black enough,
Just enough,
To sleep with a black woman…

I was in the midst of a wrinkled cream Church, to stand,
And pronounce to a fair skinned God,
That I hate black.
And yet,
At the stroke of a ginger dawn,
That broke,
And yet broke in sooty lightning,
I finally knew,
I really was,
Black enough,
To sleep with a black woman.

10 Sylvia

This headache,
Is madness.
It sifts through my fingers-
A movement that obeys to water
A movement that swims the Pacific
Traveling in drops;
Recounting deceit
Another failed Summer Story,
A fairytale that ends in the girl with the Red Hood.

A migraine has been wedding my skin,
Bedding my fingers;
The poetry came from somewhere else-
Within me, I am stronger than you.

The strength weans at your thoughts,
Somehow I have inadvertently borrowed your thoughts,
Yet it seems like someone must have conspired,
For when sadness binds sadness,
New atoms are born.

Your life was so sad.
And your death so beautiful
There's something so melancholic about a young death.
Your smile was summer
Your death winter
I was born in winter.

I think everyday this headache deepens
I get a little madder
You were so sad Sylvia
The electricity and the children
And the cheating jealous husband
Why were you so sad?

Has it flown?
This swiftness stops me.
My lips glue to opium farms.
My roots bow down to your roots.
My coldness echoes your eyes.

There is a place
It is brown and snow makes it grey
It parts a little whenever you smile
It breaks a little
The crevices so beautiful in their autumn like death
This place
Oh it rambles too.
But it fractures at happiness
I am not sure
If that is just denial
Or a consumed-ordinary human being.

My madness subsides with technology
I lose you at times.
I occasionally find you in a song or two
The sadness comes back for a moment
There is a place
Where you live
It's dichotomous that I'd want to persist with a migraine

But what a beautiful migraine you are
There's something so hypnotic
So powerful in sadness
I can breathe through yours and almost call it mine
Trying to cover up those fractures from that place
That had started to wear out
That had yellowed like turmeric
And is sulphur now.
As I had found a shade lighter
Amalgamating
The commonness in sadness

Sadness is imperial
It shall numb you
But it shall awe you and you shall melt like a slave
You shall want to become that place
The place that gets lighter and lighter with despair
Till it is pitch white
And the streets get so dark
That only few can relish it
That only people like us can understand it
People like us?
Strangers bound by a timeless suicide
A nostalgic sadness of colonial embraces
A cerebral disillusionment
Beautiful syllabic madness
People
Who transcend and meet at a secret place only sadness knows of
People
Who die
And people who are born in winter. ■

11 Sleepwalking in Seattle

Droning,
In heavy lavender scented chunks,
And lumps;
Liam,
I am sleeping to you.
Thank you.

Thank you,
For the Lancashire and Manchester buildings
Of ash coloured mud,
Baked bricks,
And steel toys,
That entertain on command.

Command fear,
Command stature.
Adorn a proletarian village,
Far, far away,
In the mystical land of unaware elephants,
Snake charmers,
Tea and cowardice…
Ignorance and deception…
Oh, Liam!
You have been pushing around your,
Nylon love.
You have been a cupid to the land.

You have landed more than you have borne,
And you have brought me exotically carved shawls,
Colours,
Adventure and pre-renaissance enjoyments,
And made them all justifiable.

You have justified yourself,
Injected a lullaby to the yellow rivers of sorrow…
Liam,
Why do I believe you?

I believe you,
For it's true.
For our ballroom dances,
Are more than simple movements,
For there is so much smoke,
That cotton can't plug it,
There is so much wetness,
That cotton can't soak it.

Cotton can't soak it Liam.
Thank you.
You gave me a revolution.
When our poor, poor, rustic neighbours,
Were so down,
Bristling their handsome knees,
On a tarry land,
Hoping to play a game,
Of hide and seek,
With deep buried potatoes.

Liam,
There you are.
With a rock the size of your heart.
Smiling at me at flavoured tea parties and tennis courts.
Playing cricket with railways,
That you have made,
Out of frustration.
Steam engines and burning coal,
All conspiring with the Queen,
To foster you ahead.

Thank you,
Liam.
I am sleeping to you.
Holding in my mittened hands,
The ends of my white frilled gown.
In a frenzied Dust Bowl,
And an Irish migrated Farmville,
I guess I shall marry you,
For I thank you.
For I,
Am sleepwalking in a slavish brothel,
That feeds you soft wheat,
And shuts your mouth for once,
When you take a bite and chew,
The left over pleasures,
Of a sleeping Seattle. ■

12 The Man I Lost to Technology

I am your wife; remember?
You signed a square white page with me,
And you used an ordinary blue pen.

You gave me a chunk of a stone,
That gleamed only in the hand, never in my eyes,
You never went to a dinner alone.
Still there was no substance in the crevice.

We were in Venice.
(At least I was)
Once there used to be Venus and Adonis,
Now everything is a thirty-year -old's Santa Claus.

Where were you that time?
When I was dragging along with me, lurked beneath my Maybelline smile; a body,
I had somehow, killed in an invisible crime;
(It was supposed to be a honeymoon with Baccardi)

We were both sleeping.
But you snored.
I gathered a lot of hollow irritation, set the calm reaping,
And filled your pillow with cotton till it soared.

A red tie,
I gifted you on your birthday.

You replied with a twinkle in your eyes.
It was the last thing you tried to say.

A boat with champagne.
Men and women from all walks of life.
Then there swayed a tiny waste, tapping in the rain.
She called for you but you had a wife.

The next morning you opened the door.
With eyes so awake I almost loved you then.
I had been wet in the downpour.
I had been drinking till seven.

You looked at me with eyes so remote.
So sympathetic.
I wished I could go back on the same boat.
Drown or suffocate myself in the attic.

There were flashes of a yellow curry,
Some bell pepper and a charcoal pan,
I asked you not to hurry.
Within me, I ran.

Somewhere we started making everything a mess.
The food burnt that night.
We started communicating via SMS.
I opened my fist and through it trickled down a light.

We didn't abuse.
We existed.
There was always music or movies to amuse.
The routine was never evicted.

Somewhere we forgot.
We forgot we smiled.
There was always the laptop or the I-pod.
And there were desktops where files were piled.

One evening,
I saw the rouge sun set.
It blushed and I remembered our beginning.
A tear crept down my cheek; it said you lose the greenery of the grass you get.

I silently ascertained the thought.
I felt a pang down my throat.
I really forgot.
I should have done something, Maybe gifted you a new coat.

It's human to err.
I wanted to be divine.
I let the truth smudge and blur.
The mistake was as much yours as you were mine.

I wanted to hurt you.
Literally.

Were things dirtier than dirt too?
How the hell could you not notice the ring on my belly?

And such a pretty face,
You perfectly managed to avoid,
Losing out to a delusional race,
And drilling too deep, a disgusting void.

I wanted you to surrender.
Hands up. Head over heels.
Then walk all over you and your gender.
To let you know what vanity feels.

The clouds were soft on my feet,
When you were fading.
Then I smelled a faint perfume of defeat.
It was a lullaby. I was cascading.

Folks were fools.
For love was being personified.
I was being hushed by a fire that cools.
It resurrected what had died.
I woke up with a scream.
And looked at the side of my bed, a dazed glare,
(What a sour dream!)
You were not there.

I slapped you, kissed you and then stoned you in my imagination.

Anything- to bring you back.
You have stepped beyond my emotional nation,
With every new piling file on the rack.

I have been things.
Things that suppress you.
And I don't know whenever the doorbell rings,
If there is need for an apology?
There is silence if I want to caress you.
Are you the man I lost to technology?

What are you doing these days?
I still sit in the garden chair,
And think of all that the quiet says.
With that I hope to hear you somewhere.

And as I sip down my tea,
I remember the gleam I saw in your eye the day I was drunk.
Did I make it up in a head so drowsy?
Or was it then that the reality should have sunk.

I didn't care that time.
And now, I just wonder.
The evening starts to sublime.
The light slips under.

Not long ago.
I wanted to inflict you with a knife.
What happened in between? I guess I shall never know,
But you know, I am supposed to be your wife.

A breath is now a boon,
The diamond moistens my eyes and sings a song to me,
I wail in my dreams, climb up the moon-
-With a staircase where you belong to me.

Then I stir from my infant fantasy.
No angel arrives.
There is a tarnished ecstasy.
Machines again enslave our lives.

You come home.
I reach for you.
I clasp but air. Is it an obsessive syndrome?
I want to reach for you.

I try to think of you, your life.
After all, I am your wife.
Then I stand frozen.
Concentrate.
Oranges, Milk, Soup, Grapes, 20 rupees a dozen.
I see confusion swiftly evaporate.
And think of a stranger.
That I married. ■

13 Throne

Your mouth opens,
Only to close,
At the flush of,
Hysteria,
Drugs-
Hysterical drugs.
Your mouth,
It twinkles.
The lines around it fold,
Then flatten,
Then fold,
Carving a niche,
Of their own;
Sarcasm,
And fortune- tellers.
They mime,
Dummy songs of freedom.
You protest,
In veils.
Your thoughts,
Splatter.
Sometimes,
You breathe.
The rest of the times,
You rule. ■

14 Diwali

A bucket of oil,
And a mound of earth,
I burn you,
With shredded bits of paper,
A notion of festivity,
Crumpled by the genuineness of rains,
I burn you,
With all that misguides me.
When the sun shines,
Celebrations cease.
It's the dark,
Which simulates mimicry,
Huh, that stupid sun.
I burn you,
With all that the orange idiot brings.
There is smoke,
It's like a snake,
With neon shades....
Cyclically,
Flesh burns,
Cyclically,
A bucket of oil hangs,
Coins, like empty vessels,
Make noise.
Every year,
Something sweet floats on my tongue,
Every year,
I burn you.

15 Foreigners

Maybe it's the thought.
Maybe you don't recognize my language.
You can touch my daughter,
Rip apart my sons,
My words shall just echo
Against your splendid walls,
And enchant you with that exotic accent.
You shall objectify my words,
Ogle through them,
Maybe touch me a little too,
You wouldn't recognize my language.

You shall slit open my house,
Tear down my clothes,
Not bother to clean up for the siege,
Not having to answer,
Not having to hear,
Desperately, irately looking in me,
For malignancy,
Or something at least,
Otherwise you shall subside with,
The plain old sedition-
You shall stud my picture on your shining armour,
Like you're doing me a huge favour
And infect me with vendors.

You shall dissect my existence,
Upturn my currency,
Terrify your wafer thin mind,
And give it a good little shake,
And then one-track it like you've been doctored to,
Like your nation,
Festooned upon by natural calamities,
Is a man-made disaster itself,
Oh, how your mind frizzles;
Yes, I shall protest
And you shall rub your mind a little harder now-
When the house wreck or the spite-filled violation won't work,
You shall turn to those big fat Interpreters,
But since you are on a pig race,
Your mind is sure to get swine flu,
And yes, as sharing as you are,
You shall bestow it upon the rest of us,
But you won't really listen to what I have to say,
The easier my elimination, the more patriotic you shall be.
But what if,
One day all your bubbles shall explode,
Pulling along those nail-size nations as you trip,
Trip badly,
And all your Interpreters lose their jobs,
Will your glorious little brain care to decipher my words?

Or just leave it there, fending for itself,
Fighting off fingers that offset paranoia?
Will you sit down for a moment?
Look me in the eye,
Hear?
Before you sentence me to a lifetime of slavery,
Dungeons of autocracy,
And iron bars of hypocrisy,
I think you should,
Go and learn my language first.
For there are too many fidgety illiterates rampaging about,
Trying to suppress what they don't understand. ■

16 Littlest Finger

She holds mine.
Hers: one fourth of mine.
A gush of canned warmth,
Suddenly punches me.
A television-rainstorm,
Wets me.
Somehow,
I don't smile.
Somehow,
She doesn't realize.

Mine coloured.
Mine creamed.
Hers;
Softer.
Mine,
Helping,
Scribbling dishes,
Scratching pens,
Pressing clothes,
With paper harsh,
Wood-smooth
Palms.
Taking another gulp of routine,
Hers are locked in mine.
Somehow,

I don't smile.
Somehow,
She doesn't realize.

Strangers,
Like sunlight,
Enter both our doors.
She's not the same anymore.
Off to a new road of reality,
That's tougher to penetrate
Than the fantasy world of dolls;
She still holds mine.
Now, it's the same size.
And I feel as if a bucket
Of bullets
Wets me inside.
Somehow,
I don't smile.
Somehow,
She doesn't realize.

Today she holds another.
Her grin stretches like the horizon.
Her eyes shine.
But I don't know if
She needs me,
Or she misses me,
Or just lights up

At the glimpse of the pink rock,
Next to hers,
Or compares it
To the white dot of my ring finger.
Mine is freckled now,
With age studded on jutting out veins,
And creases,
Creases everywhere…
And today, she also holds mine.
And spectacularly,
No feeling descends,
No feeling ascends,
A feeling that was there,
Since she was born,
Speaks to me,
And stays there.
Somehow,
She smiles,
Somehow,
I don't realize.
There is a gulp in the throat,
A hiccup,
And all that,
That rested on,
And then deserted,
My littlest finger.

17 Traumatic Diamonds

Black and blue,
They beat me down,
I am snuggling a crude ground,
With prestige dripping down my armpits,
In a sweat,
That is perfumed to lure.
And lure it does,
I am no more animal than human.

True blue moon romances,
Bartered and traded on fingers,
And rings, rings, rings.
My romance is my weakness.
They say they are your best friends.
They are my weakness,
They capture so wildly that I can't breathe,
It's so sweet,
That I cant put it in words,
It's like a chariot full of petunias,
Or sweeter.

They compete with books,
But then books need patience,
And shunning vanity.

And no woman in her senses,
Is man enough to let go,
Of Eros for platonic picnics.

And just when I am about to surrender civility,
For the feel of them,
I find myself black and blue.

Oh My God!
I think they are sluts. ■

18 Morality/Too Much and Always..

Overflowing with emotion,
She's tanning away my dreams.

Overbearing confusion
And overwhelming sleep drives me beyond,
Beyond the realm of God
And conscience.
And in one go,
I lose them both.

Softening my already slim chances,
Of finding my way back,
Back home.
I know not what shall happen.
And in a masked happening,
I hope to never see her irritating smile again.
Donning a fox skin,
And a poppy love,
I shall rather not talk about it.

While she's painting her nails
And I am painting her black,
She is breaking my frame.
Crash.
And with a noise of a hollow vessel,
She's winning the chess like game.
And then I wink.
And she becomes my napkin.

I use her.
Slandering the way through a miracle,
She's mint now.
Green and dewy.
And I am the sun
Who crystallizes the mud.
She's sprouting my dreams,
On gravity.
And I am illuminated,
Flashing my orbit teeth from the sky,
I spread an epidemic.
They call it light.
And I am older now,
But I sparkle anyhow.
She's in the west.
I set on her.

Towering notions,
Split me into two.
What's my ethnicity now?
Is it with me? Faded, uncertain?
Or has it become fatalistic?
She's coming around again,
And she's a needle.
She nips me.
And now I am a deflated gas balloon.
And she's tanning my dreams,
Always obstructing the way,
Congealing the vision-
I know why she lost out to smoke,
And cyanide.
She used to win too much.

Freezing, solidifying,
I see her turn blue,
And she suffocates my dream,
While air elopes and colour erodes
From her skin,
And I see pavements of blood trickle down the corners of her smile,
And settle on her dimples
Permanently.
And that's when I strangle her mind
And try and squeeze out my dream.

But nothing moves.
And then I see my clothes.
Soiled in a plethora of splintered portions,
They silently live
And I know where I belong.
And then I need her.
For I am incredible dirty,
And water doesn't wash away my blots.

Wishing and waltzing with time,
Once a month,
I cry out in my sleep.
Flustered. Frustrated.
I commiserate a burnt dream,
Submitting to her;
Too much and always. ■

19 Hiccups

Dreams are minor hiccups,
Choking every inch of your throat,
With knots,
Bloody knots,
Of breathless,
Panting, social benchmarks.

My dream was you.
My dream,
Was like a smudged oil pastel,
Replete with improper lines,
Asymmetrical heart aches,
Dementia,
Pale, listless hero-worship,
Submission,
Scapegoat sacrifices.
My dream,
Died.

My dream was a house.
A house,
Like the butterscotch cones,
Symmetry all over,
Perfect shapes,
Absolutism,
Sane,
Sound,
Perfectly parabolic smiles.
The house,
Burnt.

My dream,
Was a silver lining,
In the scorching sunlight,
My dream,
Was strong.
It was a rope,
You could pull up,
And draw water from wells from,
It was,
Like a nail,
On a coffin,
Never letting the death,
Escape its confinements.
My dream,
Sublimed.

Dreams,
Parting waves,
Ripples,
Reality and feasibility,
Get to me.
Dreams,
Entwined in my tongue,
Deafen me.
Dreams,
Engulf me,
Twitching,
And itching a little.
Dreams,
They are hiccups.
They pass. ■

20 Cremation And Its Contemporaries

A grey note,
I am grey.
He loses a vote,
He loses a prey.

All is but what it seems.
You didn't give me colour.
And you didn't make any darkness creams.
It's better to have a dark identity than an ashen pallor.

Ashen pallor.
He immersed me in the Ganges.
Chaste.
And thought I'd purify.
Purify,
Haha.

Haha,
He doesn't know.
I am but a cigarette.
I burn smoke.
Spreading black oranges,
Selling a blue yellow flame,
In a market,
Where he is so lost.

Where he is so lost,
That he is unconscious.
He has money,
But he doesn't buy,
What I offer.
He hates me.

He hates me.
So he tries hard to rub me.
But he doesn't realize,
He is rubbing against a tray.
He hopes to null my fire.
He loses a vote.
He loses a prey.
I turn to ash.

I turn to ash,
But the fire doesn't die.

The fire doesn't die.
It transcends. ■

21 Dear Moms and White Lies

She grows back in time,
Your mother cries.
Fairies are escapes.
Santa Claus has white hair.
A white flowing gown.
A veil.
And wine and a wedding.
A beautiful wife.
A beautiful smile.
Your mother cries.
You were brought up with cornflakes.
And a school bag of lies.
Rolling eyes and scrutinizing frowns.
A water bottle of neglect.
You loved waving her goodbye.
Your mother cries.
You were told everything was happy.
Home sweet home.
Ghosts vanish in the light.
Why does your mother cry?
You grew up to believe,
That Mom was a fairy and Dad, your Santa.
But Santa has white hair.
And fairies want to escape.
You shut your eyes.
It's bedtime.
Time turns over.
There is always a cherub in the story.
Happy ending.
You shut your eyes.
Your mother cries.

22 Gypsum (Once In a Blue Moon)

Whitewash the moon,
There are
Way too many
Scars and sour-cream mountains,
Pale sulphur greyness,
Imperfections;
Lingering, diffused,
Carbon-ash pigments.
The work of an immature craftsman,
Which infects the rituals of the eyes,
Inflames the iris,
And flickers the pupil.
Well, whitewash it then.

For all you know,
You might even succeed.
Conquer a Poison Ivy of sweet lime lakes,
Depose the autocracy of an imperfect Natrium shade,
Which erupts from solar thrones.
Whitewash it, then.

The subtle imaginary line,
Equatorial tanneries,
And tropical summers,
Won't be brown-

The copper earth will turn tinny,
Frozen,
And not be the orange carrot nose
on a white Snowman,
Instead,
All will blend,
And pour more white, white,
White lies,
-If you whitewash the moon.

Selene will tranquilize,
Die, in a jiffy of quagmire,
Or maybe Cynthia will wipe it out with a fire.
Slowly, all things will fizz out,
And acid remains will trickle down,
The mittens of beauty.
There shall be no more of it,
For there shall be all of it.
Or just a holy wing,
And an olive branch of floodlight,
Monochromatic, white,
Chalk-corrected,
Moonlight,
Faceless, shapeless,
No fairies, no craters-
The day you whitewash the moon;
Floodlight, in the eyes,

Chalk, corrected moonlight,
Children won't be afraid of the dark.
They will grow up, fearless,
Adult, baggy shouldered before they trigger
Consonants and alphabets
And dream of a black Witch spinning wheel on
A pigmented moon.
Chalk, corrected moonlight,
Floodlight.
Floodlight,
Chalk, corrected,
Moonlight.
The day you whitewash the moon,
No more things,
Will happen,
Once,
In a blue moon. ■

23 Tiaras

You hold records;
A seminar of expeditions
That circumvent
And destroy
A puffed up part
Of the magic act-
The preface mirrors your vanity,
Resurfaces your various plastic dents,
Scars and patches,
It's magical,
How real it seems;
The puffed up part,
Is almost the size of your palm;
Restructuring your palm,
And the various criss-crosses,
That formed because you used to close your fists often,
For you used to think too much.
What did thoughts come down to?
This beautiful magic,
That transcended into you,
A beautiful synthetic-you.
A new chemical,
Spectacular,
Glistening,
Clenched in your fist,
A puff,
That dissolves.

24 Battles

Crazy metaphors;
Raining cardboard hearts
On grounds so slippery
That you lose the gravity to a blanket of
Banana peels,
You lose.

Crazy metaphors;
Hide and seek,
A drop of red,
A drop of white,
A tangent of lies
To a circle of rings.
Dragging your violated skin,
Across floors so crooked
That you lose your ground.
You lose.

Crazy metaphors;
Juxtaposition of coal mines and ruggedly
Sensual solitaires,
Sub Saharan skins
Drenched in a flood of light,
Dry up,
On lands so unfamiliar
That they lose their thirst.
They lose.

Crazy metaphors,
Graveyards resonant of last names,
Plastered on limp voices,
With a permanent ink
So red,
It's darker than blood.
-Not dying alone,
Yet always haunted by a shadow you're tied to,
With a rope so plastic
That you lose not just that insipid life,
But, also your death.
Losing.
Losing.
Losing words.
Faces.
Such synonyms.
There are,
Such losers. ■

25 Murder, Murder

Two hands met,
In a pale, yellow fainting porch light,
Twilight and its remnants,
Aching them a little,
A chilly sensual wind,
Trembling them a little,
Like a nervous first move,
A puppy love from a distance,
They met.
Someone sighed,
Then droned,
The breath deepened,
In heavy doses,
It came rhythmically,
Panting,
A muffled shriek,
A faint reddening scar on the neck,
And then it quietened.
The hands had met,
Sparking all that remained,
Numbing all that chilling curiosity,
In the monotone of the merge,
The hands had met,
Like they had always dreamed of,

The fingers were hard,
The clasp eternal,
They had met,
And left their marks lingering.
Lingering in the paleness of colourless thoughts,
Blackened dreams,
Charred portions of a fading, faking love.
The hands had met,
Someone had sighed.
The deed was done.
The girl was dead. ■

26 Nails

In a platter of waste,
The un-needed rest.
Ringing bells,
With dirty winds,
From time to time.
The winds,
Dirty winds,
Are also,
Strong winds.
Blue with cold,
Bitter with frozen,
Beam balances,
Of partisan bloods.
Scratched pale,
Spotted white,
A zebra with no darkness,
Milk-less.
They lie,
Anguished,
Unkempt,
Burnt.
Stems cut off from roots,
Hunting in the ink blue light,
And hand plucked land,
For pieces,
Which grow beneath,

Roots.
Green eyed
Battered,
The wind comes in a murky fleet,
And carries with it,
Heavy suits of angst,
The same platter of nobodies,
Due west,
So west,
They gape.
And by the time,
It's morning,
They are redeemed,
Smiling, at what they made of mud-
Waste;
Such waste.
Perching on alighted erstwhile dustbowl wings of an angel,
They smile.
They are west now.
Quite west.

27 Shameless, The Lord Will Forgive You

Erotic
It slips through my vein.
Purity is for those believers
Who fear the satanic cult.
Curls hover around in toroids
Of randomness.
I desire you.
You love me.
Nah, It's not the same thing.

Hold my hand.
At three in the morning,
Walk me to your grave.
Then flow in my hair.
Please don't leave me.

Erotic
It may seem to them.
But I want you.
At the brink of my opal tears,
You are naked.
Tears unfold and unpack me,
I am your wrapper,
I hid you when they came searching for Jewish Whores,
You were not Blue-Eyed.

You are the dust,
Scattering light through a peephole
In my dark room,
I want to confiscate it.
And become filthy again;
In your arms.

I am toppling from the stars.
In twinkling comets,
I am frantically searching for you.

Erotic.
Yes, we share the same bed
As I undress your layers,
They hail me.
As I accumulate you,
Uncovered by scientific dictations,
I try to justify
Lust.

Erotic,
I still want you.
Let me melt your lips and dry your eyes.
You can't think for yourself.
Let me think for you.
Blinkered.
They name me.

But I am fumbling in your thirst.
Drink me before its dawn,
And I evaporate.
And sacrifice for me,
Soak up as my substitute.
The Lord will forgive you.

In denial, we sin.
And sit back and watch.
Erotic
Cling on me tightly,
Hold me close.
I want you pale with the yearning.
The German burning.

Erotic,
Look in the mirror,
And detest what you behold.
At three in the morning,
With hovering curls,
And Hazel eyes,
Wake me up,
Shake me,
From my slumber,
Erotic
And confess that you long for me.
Because,

Then I would desert you,

Head to my Aryan wife and leave you in pleading relinquished agony,

Begging me to reciprocate,

Erotic

I want you.

I want you nude with vacuum identity.

Merge your name with my colloidal norms.

As you fold up your hands

Tainted

Erotic,

I leave them. ■

28 Ms. Muppet

Little hands,
Of half hearted wishes…
Ms. Muppet dreams of puppets,
Moving pictures,
And cinematic vistas.
Oh have you see my Romeo?
I can't seem to find him.

A locket,
In her floral jacket,
And a lucky secret,
She shares with no one.

She desires all and everything,
So much so,
That's she pursues each,
Half-heartedly.

She hangs mud chimes,
On her ceiling,
They tell her of the knocking wind.
And the musical reunion,
Awaiting her,
Outside her door.

Ms. Muppet,
Owns a piggy bank.
She collects heartaches there.
And is happy,
To shatter it one day,
And vent them all.
Have you seen her Romeo?

Puppets, puppets on her hand,
A handful of wishes,
Pink cushions and DVDs.
The world melts,
In aristocratic lumps,
In funny fading indulgences,
Of a dying nuance,
In her little hands. ■

29 Plastic

Bated breath.
We thought you smiled.
Those fragile Ohio lips,
Twisted,
We thought a demented jest,
And a skateboard of more smiles,
Was dripping through the corners of your mouth.
Seventeen years of poignancy,
Was subliming;
And stars were killing,
To twinkle in your iris.
When you clutched our hand,
It was out of love,
It was a drop,
A sweet pickle,
Of an abberated smile.
Little did we notice,
The skateboard flip,
The hand crumple,
The smile polymerize.
Little did we see pain,
Littler death,
And the least,
Your liquid eyes,
Reproach,
Transcend,
To become,
Forever,
Our plastic eyes.

30 Saprophytes

Every language carries a message.
What's mine when you are not there?
There is a hosepipe full of war in our souls,
Blood, in a tumbler that's not mine.
Yet the blood may be mine.
What's mine when you are not there?

Empty houses,
And a peephole of flies,
No dust, no light,
There is nothing in me that would shine,
Nothing that won't,
With shrouds of hometown love,
When the hometown is mine.
What's mine when you are not there?

Every day, I whine.
You bake homes of face cards in a wind,
That twists every life it passes through,
Peephole after peephole,
Washing,
A contented doom.
The doom is not mine.
Everyday,
I try and live it through.
You earn bread that fungi decease in,
I eat bread that Mary Antoinette died for.
Everyday, we live a fungus.
Every language carries a message.
Every day,
We get close, to jugglers of words.

31 Neon Light

Stripped and restless,
It peeps,
Through the corners of his eyes,
At the corners of his eyes,
Searching in them,
Wild, impatient,
A spark,
That is now a stone.

A handful of books,
Which mourn a dying language
In his hand.
In his hand,
A sparrow of sweet talk flutters:
A bridge of grains,
Separates them,
And he hugs the world,
Homeless and hungry.

His shoulders slouch,
As the weight of promises bends him.
Speechless,
In his own house,
He hates to live
With a family of dying bones and sinking hearts,
A bat of a past,
Blind in the day,

Powerful in the night,
Engulfs and swallows them every night.

Every day,
He hopes to try,
He tries to hope,
A scar on his forehead pricks,
Frustrated,
Irritated,
He can't seize the day.
So, he marries the night.

Then he gets invited,
To a world that wants to be more,
And those light-skinned damsels,
Offer him much more than a home,
They keep a hand on his head,
But don't really touch him,
And while he holds an exhilarated squirrel in his hands,
He jumps,
Frivolously,
A bridge of water now separates them,
While the light-skinned damsels,
Put the other hand,
Seductively,
In his pocket.

Cologne,
And a sweet rich perfume,
Puts him to sleep,
While an exotic creamy hand feeds him grapes in his mouth,
And his mouth shuts,
And an accented voice hums a lullaby to him,
And he doesn't speak anymore.
He tags a foreign name on his heart,
And as they make him a globalized slave,
He doesn't complain.
It has been in his blood.

Flooded with crutches and translators,
He is almost happy,
He is indifferent to whatever grows beyond his mirror,
Or dies,
Who cares?
And,
As he goes to sleep,
On his foreign silk bed sheet,
He is restless and stripped,
And something escapes the corners of his eyes,
And his eyes seek for it,
Searching for it in every face,
That prospers.

The sparrow perches on his head now,
While the books are at his feet,
He is a squirrel, who's left with no answers.
Yet every one in his family,

Still looks up to him.
And he loses his bat eyesight,
Nothing seems poignant anymore.
In tents,
Refuges, camps, swamps,
And puddles,
He searches for something,
That lived in his eyes,
His insight is on debt,
And his soul is the exclusive menu for a suburban restaurant,
And then,
When he looks within,
There is nothing there,
Nothing,
But neon light.

Stripped and restless,
A past of no protests,
Delays, norms,
Responsibilities, missionaries,
And submission strikes him.
All bridges sublime.
And he stands with the statue of liberty,
Equally confused and torn apart,
Between a dog and a neon light. ■

32 Losing Your Mind, In A Traffic Light

Roses wilt,
And you are a shoe-flower,
With white wine spilt,
At the chrysanthemum's wailing hour,
You become the green line,
I become the red stripe.
The sunflower in a gazebo of sunshine,
Turns sick, turns ripe.
It's a lovely story; it is,
Of hometown flowers,
A milky bliss;
Chrysanthemum hours.

She comes,
Like the fairy Godmother to Cinderella,
Raining the sound of drums,
With an upturned umbrella,
And protects your orchard of dreams,
She weaves the sun,
To your wreathing seams,
And the light is now a yellow one.

Many carriages and caravans venture past,
A herd of too much of faith,
Too much of beauty to last,
Love that is a white wraith.

Then the roses wilt,
And you cry tears of silt,
It's not a love poem; this one,
For it has light and it has a sun.

My red light has spectral meanings,
In your heart of green things;
I bring to you a cold wave,
Washing over a lukewarm civil cave,
Of deep rooted wishes and subliminal desires,
That treads over shoe-flowers.

She brings to you a vista of marigold nature,
And an aphrodisiac nomenclature,
And a din of sunlight,
Splashing your obsolete wimpling might.

A curtain of yellow light to get prepared,
And a little more scared,
Hangs on her window,
With roses planted in a haphazard row,
And you are the green silk,
To her curtain,
When the white wine spills like milk,
On floral-men.
And from your weak eyes,
Of incandescent dyes,

For a blue drop to fall,
It takes a red-letter call,
For a blue drop,
Needs a red light, to stop.

It takes love to build a garden,
But, maybe God had different ideas for Eden.
And a sin was enough for humanity to foster voyages ahead,
Everything- with the colour red.
A red blot on hierarchy and leisure,
I am the tainted spot that comes with pleasure.
I revolt; repulse your green pagan mirage,
With a red-wine garage.
If I am a novel song,
I am beyond the oblong,
I am wrong,
So terribly wrong to you,
Red valentine roses don't even belong to you.

She gives you a field of gold,
Sunflowers, and you are told,
That yellow cages befit green parrots,
And I am a scarecrow for reddish carrots,
You never blush and,
Roses are blood to your Greenland.

You wrong no one,
I wrong you.
But who am I in a story of two?
You plant more shoe-flowers,
And chrysanthemums wail in their lonely hour,
When both are just phases of a transparent mirror,
What causes one to wail and the other to hinder?

More green gardens are built,
And white wines spilt,
You cry tears of silt,
Roses wilt.
And a bell tolls in your head,
And you realize; that the shoe-flowers are red. ■

33 She Had Her Time
(But I love you)

Unfinished songs,
Through your lips I sing,
A piece of someone else's mind, a farmhouse of wrongs,
And another slice on your wedding ring.

You make up a bedlam of daily diaries,
And you rush out of the door,
To a headache so fiery,
That you don't want to go back home anymore.

Life is not just a circle,
It's circles after circles, of oats,
Un-thrown water of a baby's gurgle,
Gulped down the mother's throat,
With a poignant sense of comprehension,
A funny expression, at that,
An unfinished smirk of apprehension,
A womanly smile of a bubble bath,
There is so much that's unsaid,
So much that she escapes from,
There is a solace in mourning the dead,
A deep scented nostalgia, in being the queen of the prom,
Reckless high school sweethearts,
And those thanksgiving apple tarts;

But now the apples are somehow yellow,
And her baby boy's wailings have turned mellow,
Her fetishes are all over the place,
And boredom breathes down the neck
Of an Aphrodite conjured on a missionary star trek;
There are wrinkled white frock and orange shrub dreams,
And her longing no longer screams,
Running at a speed so ruddy fast,
Indeed, good things seldom last….

You come from a home smelling of baby powder,
And Cerelac.
My song thumps louder,
And then begins to slack,
Her yellow eyes are somewhere lost,
I write a song on their suntan,
And her butterfly heart, carelessly tossed,
In a four-day-old glorified life span;
I sing through your lips,
She happens to hear it,
But then it's nobody's fault,
That a man often slips.

And then, when I look at her again,
I see no blame in her eyes, no pain.
It aches, this itchy, tacky thought,
But I rather enjoy her face.
It is not green,
It's grateful,
She hasn't really seen,

How colours are always fateful,
Mine younger than hers,
Hers compensated with bygone cocktails and furs,
Mine painting an embossed smile on a borrowed canvas,
I didn't even bother paying for,
She didn't even realize she was lending,
She had lent a blind eye for my colours to trespass,
And prevail over her door,
My colours were so condescending
That everyday her painting topples and blurs,
Mine younger than hers.

Blinded, some visions are,
She has no time to count her scars,
In a city full of borrowings and mortgages,
She hums with the passing of a fast car,
Flips through the yellow pages,
She doesn't quite notice,
Her ring slip from her fingers,
She throws her baby a helpless kiss,
The past faintly lingers,
And as he runs,
Like men often do,
She knows some things just sprint,
He can hide my perfume with a tint,
Her colours shall only grow older,
And he would keep looking over her shoulder
As if something somewhere always lacked
She sees him run, but she hasn't really seen,
She sighs and lets it go, finding sleep in the fact,
That she was once the Prom Queen.

34 Gothic Rock

But she is just that-
-A black rose,
In a frozen cross
And its principles.

-A black umbrella gown,
Brushing against the subtle gong,
That black leaves make.
As she has her black iris,
Fixed upon a night,
That grows as her solitude enchants,
A cold English winter,
The epitome of black mourning,
She breathes,
Heavily,
Black wind blows past her olive hair,
The cross is now her coffin,
Surreptitiously, a mucky silence pervades,
Her skin,
Pinched by a waxy candle,
That glows with a grey flame,
Moss enters her howling tears,
Stagnates and hybridizes,
The pyramidal brown church turns black,
It doesn't bleed,
It reproaches,
Aquiline pillars slant to the left,

For what is right is bright,
And all that is left of it,
Are shadows,
Dark and slimy,
So slimy,
They stick to her existence,
But it's funny,
For even boxes have shadows,
Lifeless bastards,
A black Persian cat serenades,
As she perches on her shoulder,
The wind slips past her alarming eyes,
And the frozen souls in the building glide,
And circle around the cross,
The truth beneath the sword,
Hides,
Behind a black satin veil,
And they say she shall be ousted,
Dusted away with rocks,
But they know not,
That she is just that,
A black rose,
In a frozen cross,
And its principles…
And they happily push her beneath a rock,
That outshines,
And the cat still whispers in loud chimes,
As they become gothic,
Between the rocks. ■

35 I Am Yours

Those stars shine too brightly.
Don't give me a kiss now.
Those stars are burning my eyes,
The cinematic monster is,
My schoolgirl-fantasy.
But schoolgirl obsessions are a thing of the past.
And those stars are entering my vision.
They must be blinding me for I can't see you.
Expensive vintage emotions,
Light up the sky,
Whether it's day or night.
Those stars are too bright.
I am a woman now.
And I am yours.
And I am levitating with those stars.
Those stars are way too bright.
Don't put them away.
Don't touch me now.
Just buy me a ticket. ■

36 Neighbours

A time turner should have done us good,
Age scrapes off my earth,
You stand agonized,
I should have been taller,
You should have been quieter.
We've always had our issues.

Your fists cup mine,
But mine are still fragile.
There is a butterfly that sucks the nectar,
I was yours.

Revenge should have done me good
My face should have tightened.
My skin hangs loose,
Your wounds deep set,
My eyes go mad,
You sigh too much.

Under the same house,
And so many beds apart,
Our questions strangle our pillows
And sweeten our sleep,
A thick dreamless sleep,
We do not dream anymore
You live too much,
And I die too much.

37 Stupidity

Stupidity on ash,
Stupidity on a placid lake-
There all the time-
Like a balloon of nitrogen,
Always there in air,
But unnoticed,
Un-sensed,
Unaware,
Burning a sky of pigeons,
With pigeons,
-you were.
Fluttering,
Or flying….
I didn't know,
Why the sun set,
Orange,
Why, silence hung on
Clouds,
Why, I never knew why I was loving you,
There was just,
A solid lake of stupidity.
A capsule of pigeons.
That, and cancer.

38 Wooden Lips, Kissing Spiders

A virtual earth,
Of mud,
Is surmounted on a cup,
Which overflows,
Love stories.
I see you,
House the virtual earth,
In your surreal eyes,
And citrus pupils.
They dilate,
A flood of insect light,
And a caravan of leafy green promises penetrates,
And I look at you.
With a poignant longing.
Love assumes different shapes.
It's an aerosol now.
No longer water.
I try to feel you.
And I clasp a virtual earth in my hand.
In lisping sounds,
Moths lick my liquid eyes.
I try to feel you.
I can't.
There is a wall between us now.
It never percolates my love.

And it's a one sided,
Topsy turvy emotion,
Squandering in the lips,
Of a bitter, bitter world,
And between us,
There is a wall,
Within us,
There is no wood,
No cellulose.
Between us,
There is a mirror.
And within us,
Spiders. ■

39 Vanity

I am an absurd little stain.
That spreads and coagulates.
And time makes me so bloody thick,
That I can't even let my notions in.
I lock up the morning sun in a closet.
It's always night with me.
Ripe and supple.
I take a bite.
And then after twelve
I become heavy;
Heavy enough to rise.

Although I drank the night,
I am not giddy.
I see a glimmering coin.
I think it's meant for me.
But I don't pick it up.
I am not sure.
Black and white?
I can choose.
Grey is not in my tea cup.
And then I wait unknowingly;
For a white horse to come,
Carry me to Snow White forests,
Or Cinderella castles.
And that's when I smile.
I pick up the coin.

Slowly the weight becomes the space.
And yet it is pulled down.
A reddish autumn spreads on my body.
A tinge of blush.
A tried and tested stare.
And now I am a bucket;
Fetching water-
Quenching a thirst they don't think I feel.
But feel I do.
And then I plunder in the pond-
A crimson conundrum for the society.
They can't understand why I am doing this.
But I wait.
I wait for a hidden frog to come from Neverland,
And urge me to turn him into a prince.
And then I smile,
And dip my feet in the pond.

Finally I almost receive what I revered.
But surprisingly,
I struggle for words
That respect gravity
And touch the ground.
But what comes out is a retard-
Half baked gesture.
And it's still in flight
With a halo
That's moonlike.
The only reason it shines
Is because it gulped down the night.
And then I shut my eyes to the world.
But I still don't know who I really am.

I hear my heart beat.
And I sleep.
And they fear
That I may be cursed.
They suggest I wait in a chamber
And await that stranger to kiss me to life.
And then I smile
And I open my eyes.

I hear adoration.
Music.
Rapture.
Jubilation.
And it's a little confusing.
There is this white wall
With a non inertial frame.
I stick my chin up there.
And it stands out.
And then it becomes this stain.
That spreads.
That pauses.
That runs.
That glows from a distance.
And then solidifies
Into triviality
Social absurdity
Bittersweet seduction
Womanhood
Grey temples
Metaphors
And nothingness. ■

40 Arteries

Deep seated,
Invisible
Cigars
Sans tobacco,
Sans smoke,
Just blood,
Mere blood,
Crimson
And burgundy smells;
Like the coffee farms
And the cocoa seeds are never fair,
Till you pour milk,
And it shimmers
Boiling a pothole,
In a petty kettle.
Like they are old men,
On benches of tattered wood,
Silent and ginger,
Under lampposts
And silent longings;
They are deep,
Deep seated…
And if they rupture,
You lose bubbles
To the skies,

(but it's the skies that they have come from)
Like the rains,
On car vipers-
Washed away
And erupting again,
Like a migraine in the river,
That splits water into two,
Like God,
Splits into stones;
They are invisible,
Invisible...
The Columbus of a pumping organ,
The size of a fist,
Like the love of a repressed mother,
They are coiled inside,
Eyeing,
And never emerging,
Stuck in pieces of skin,
Sewed to the flesh of time,
Like a beautiful boat,
That was built,
A boat,
That never sailed. ■

41 Fan

There is a circle inside a circle,
They call it eternal,
There is a circle inside a circle,
And there is a lot of science filled inside it.

There are lots of entangled wires of Physics,
And chords and hard and ugly metal,
Giving it its spherical shape.

The Physics inside it may be imperative,
But it certainly isn't attractive,
It's so pathetic, that it is completely hidden,
Almost invisible,
So invisible the toddlers don't even see it.
Yet, it is a part of the sphere.

The sphere suspends three hands,
The hands resemble the clock,
But they don't move time,
They move air.

Instigating comfort, convenience and all other words
in the dictionary that mean the same,
The sphere is rightly placed at the top,

But perhaps, Science fails to provide beautiful faces to its expansions,
For not a single eye admires the eternal-mechanical sphere.
Probably, it's the only thing that hangs from the height,
Where others strive to be,
And yet,
It's the only thing,
That knows how secluded it feels,
To be on the lonely pole,
How lunatic it is,
To go on and on and on,
On the command of a miniscule finger,
And maybe,
It's the only thing,
God shall never listen to-
For Science,
Denies God.
And maybe,
It'll always hang there;
A circle within a circle.

42 Damascus

Damascus.
That's how you vanished.
A magic trick,
A swish of some sharp-sensuous words,
Hiding from the rain,
Dying and bleeding with vacant-satiated eyes,
In the rain-shadow
Of Damascus.

So many faces.
So many folks.
You assimilate
A juxtaposition of conflict,
Clashes,
The bronze age,
The treaties,
Go back to the realms of war,
You voice blood,
Your voice is blood,
Like The War of The Kings,
The debated
Yet acknowledged
Damascus.

You have been so much.
Blinded by so many things.
The chair and the jewel

Of their eye.
Your hands tremble.
In a wind that doesn't even blow,
Just stands still
And threatens.
You tremble,
But your hands bleed sweat,
Paranoia,
Spliced up ideals,
Like an engulfed,
Bleeding and dwindling
Under the falcon arms of
Alexander,
Damascus.

You walk on paths
Where people get visions,
Struck like lightening,
To transcend to different spheres.
You walk,
But you tip toe.
Your feet twist,
Bend
And bleed,
Slitting those puffed up veins,
And bleeding,
Bleeding faith,
And bandaging
Damascus.

That's how far you've gone. ■

43 Hearsay

I don't have a heart I'm told,
My hands are soaked in a wasted blood,
That's not just thicker than water,
But also wooden doors.
I am a tree house.
Hanging at a pseudo height.
Embracing a saprophytic air,
I am still.
They climb and trespass on me.
Through bamboo slits,
I smile.

I am not an Ill-wisher.
I am not a Well-wisher I am told.
But I see a silvered well,
That has chasms after chasms.
They throw a coin in it.
Fake silver.
And wish.
But I am not a Well-wisher.
I am somewhere.
Grey and blue.
Peacocks die there.
I go berserk and ardently search beneath crescent graves,

Your existence.
There was a gun.
That shot me at two sides.
Passed through my chest,
But never reached my heart.
They were shocked.
They questioned science and superstition at the same time.
They created havoc and riots.
They examined my yellow veins.
They penciled my natal chart.
But silly fools.
They forgot;
I don't have a heart. ■

44 Go. Went. Gone

A green slate,
Was what she left me,
Three peas on a steel plate,
Was what she left me.
Emerald green,
Then jade,
Three tears on my silver machine,
It was a green raid,
Or a jarring age,
My life,
Or promises,
Or a memoir-cage,
Five howling wolves-
Rampantly using flashlights,
To find the umbilical cord-
She had left.
She had left,
My broom shriveling,
Dust like stars-
Twinkling in the night
With lichens
And snoring big fat wolves,
Hallucinating pales of water,
Dreaming of Poseidon,

A faithful limp,
Greying middle-aged dog,
Dreaming of Aphrodite,
And a moist wrinkled curve of the lips.
As a hundred thousand unmade beds,
Crumpled soggy clothes,
Mufflers all shades of the stem,
Cushions plastered,
With moist yellow liquid,
And a moist wrinkled curve of the lips,
She had left.
A few dimes of feudalism,
A trauma-
All shades of the stem,
A spoonful of bitter spinach,
Fell on a green slate,
She had left.
She had left,
Her coffin green,
My heart brown,
My fate famished
In couplets of a green town.

45 Sally

Smart people come together.
Peanuts gulped down,
With bitter syrup.
Oh Sally!
You had to gulp down,
A syringe of motherhood.
Then milk,
And cigarettes.
Bitter syrup.
Oh Sally!
Smart people come together.
You were the peanut,
People were allergic to.
Oh Sally!
Don't come to me.
You are blonde.

46 Winters

You don't touch me anymore.
Frozen pistols lie on the table you once smashed,
Bullets made of glaciers that don't float,
An obsession that bleeds through unicorns and centaurs,
You were mine.
What happened then?

My breath freezes your stench,
I'm afraid if I exhale,
I might lose you to the air,
You shall fissure into air,
Blend into conundrums you love to craft,
You are coffined inside words,
Words others say,
Words that cushion you from my heart,
Words that press the cushion against your Pinocchio nose,
Words,
That stifle.

I still remember you looking out of the window,
The snow etching your silhouette against the glass,
A fog almost like a comet,
Flying away from me,
Towards a world I did not recognize

And you surrendered to.
Your empty eyes were on a street freshly raided,
Rampant with footsteps,
Strange faces and more winter.
I stared at you for hours that day.
Something emptied me that night.
I didn't know that it'll take a bucket full of tears,
And a fistful of centuries,
For my children to be able to rise again.
It might have been poppies.

Strangers fought that winter.
They quarrelled and bickered and slaughtered each other
Outside our window.
Your eyes never quite left the spectacle,
You later came to relish
And venerate.
The battle was won by a stranger who became more familiar
Each passing winter.
He knocked on our door one day,
You welcomed him like civil men welcome guests.
He had said that he came to barter.
We believed him like civil families believe victors.
By then, you were already beginning to solidify.
You didn't touch me that night.
And you coiled to a side,
With fringes of notions,

Notions where you clenched your God in your fist,
Frowned at me like a child,
And turned away.
And then it began to snow in our house,
The brown wood became white,
Covered heavily under thick layers of powdered rain
That left heavy traces on our doormat,
And deeper footprints on my volatile heart.
Fleece covered our mouths,
Your vicious eyes stead fast on something that no longer lived outside our window,
We were forbidden to kiss.
Not that we kissed anymore.
Hard times, winters are.
I blamed the season for the whitewash of my civilization.
It seemed that you had been built up by assembling pieces of ice.
Ice melts in heat.

Slowly, things at home started rupturing.
You came home so lost,
So colourless,
It seemed like you had been painted by chalk.
You cracked the glass that wanted to warm you,
You broke the lights that made you blink,
Desperate to preserve the ghost that you had become,
Mimicking the stranger who was flocking our winters,

You upturned the table where I sat.
And everything you devastated,
Lay still,
Slit open,
Wounded and bleeding,
Nurturing blood,
Streamlining blood,
On subtle sidewalks of our hearts, that had begun to separate us,
Dripping,
Soaking, and crying blood,
Under a siege
Of dirty, raping blood.

I wish I could shut the realm of my eyes
And let the strangers in my life pass
Like dust passes through a peephole of light,
Except that there's no light,
Just cold wars,
Indifference.
Difference.
And you.

The stranger violates our home.
He lifts up his finger and you delude.
Your eyes become brittle.
When I come to you,
You turn to the Gods.

And you are like a sticky reflection of water,
When poured in a cauldron of disbelief,
You begin to doubt.
You fragment all the mirrors we built together,
There is no reflection anymore;
Just cold waves, frost bites and funerals of sound.
You fracture my lips with a hammer you borrow from him,
You squeeze the iridescence in me and tie me to a rope.
You kiss me today,
But you kiss me in spite.
Trying profusely to paint me into something else,
Your lips are the instrument to the abstract,
The brush to your art.
You paint me red,
So bloody red,
That I almost become a proud part of the gallery of things that you shattered,
And you just sit there,
Look into me with those ghastly insipid eyes.
And you smile.

Bathed in red,
I'm a thorn in your cemetery.
The stranger owns you now.
He fiddles with the strings that stimulate you.
You abandon me with your remains, your ruins,
Your stench and your spite.

And carry with you my nothing.
Yet, I cannot stop loving you.
There is a waft of tears,
A divorce of colours,
And memories of a haunting stranger,
You travel alone,
Stepping across,
To a world that's not yours,
Leaving a world that was,
And it's funny, that I still remain a part of yours,
And though your God,
Is different from my God,
He still stays with me.
These are things,
You shall never understand. ■

47 Foggy Breakfast

It's a foggy breakfast,
But there is a sifting ray of the pink sun,
We are in a place where shadows don't cast,
And hand in hand with hope we run.

In a forest which is colloidal,
It's still a foggy breakfast,
In a pair of eyes that are abysmal,
An aromatic memory shall always last.

It's a shady room,
And it is patched with bittersweet instances,
As a bird alights towards sonic boom,
A man cleans his lenses,
Not prophesying the blunder,
His blurred vision transfixed on something far away,
Suddenly realizes that he is looking at her,
He turns away.

But it's a foggy breakfast,
She walks on,
A dilapidated bicycle of the past,
When there used to hang a smile for every dawn.

It's Christmas,
He announces,
As soft bells murmur without fuss,
You are man and wife now, the man in white pronounces.
It's a muffled romance,
Chiming in her ear,
The moon has feet that sway in a nocturnal dance,
She wishes him a happy new year.

The night sleeps on her heart,
She awakens to a dewy morn,
Privations encased, time wheels the cart,
Despite the spectacles worn,
It's still a foggy breakfast,
Remembrance is yet another word,
The ship sails without the mast,
The fish swims with the bird.

We are in a place where shadows don't cast,
Searching for relief,
She is a lonely creature.
It snows till the lights last,
Her mind upturns hushed furniture.

Their story drowns with the Titanic,
The afternoon walks over their past,
But he turns away, the girl shrieks in panic,
It's just a foggy breakfast. ■

48 Reasons

Could I tell you why
You won't treat me anymore.
You cannot treat me anymore.
I've gathered my disease in a fist,
Dressed it on a spoon,
Wiped the spoon clean with froth, foam, water,
A rugged cloth that smelled like you,
And lifted it up through my fingers that had infected your dreams,
And folded my fingers the way you fold them
And get caned on your knuckles by 'Axis teachers'.
And while my fingers were creased and posed,
My breath was hanging frozen in time like the cadavers you preserve in ice,
And while my breath was halted,
My eyes blinked like Jesus would have blinked when he was born without a sperm-
And I sighed like you must have sighed when I married you,
And then my nose twitched like your nose twitches when you treat those widows,
And my cheeks feigned red like your hands do when you plunge them into someone's skin,
I moved my fingers and put the disease in my pocket and soaked it in my skin like I soak your dipping dirty soiled white coats,

And then something strange happened.

My lips moved and parted like they part when you look into the tunnels of my throat with your funny torch.

But this time,

They sired sound.

And the disease invaded on my soul like pharmacy invades your mind,

And the disease slowly sucked out my depths,

Digging inch by inch, like you had upturned my layers,

And then covered me with a social cello tape.

And that's when I knew I had been ailing.

With the weight of the iron clad, bickering world with many a hands, fingers and forceps like you,

It's too huge a risk, too close to the borderlines of crime,

To be in love.

So I realize what I have done to myself like you realize that it's easier to spill pity than spit love,

It is then that I realize,

That you will not treat me anymore.

Doctors are forbidden in this kingdom of jellied sentiments, maladies, and sounds,

Such sounds. ■

49 Through The Glass Wall

Blue bells
And you die.

A beautiful, beautiful life,
Spent with daisies and white hill white flowers,
Pollens hidden beneath a cloak of air,
Heaving for drops of Godliness.

A patchy face,
Altercations of the night,
Grey cells and a cell of bricks,
It's too much,
Just too much,
To contain.

You sit in a corner,
A square corner,
Dripping sweat.
And thoughts.

Drizzling from your mouth,
An acid famishes your thirst.
Colour gains torque.
And you are on the pavement,
Of insanity.

You go into a forest of chocolate,
Daily life and mashed potatoes,
And romantic tablespoons.
And a furor of blue engulfs you.
You reach home.
A bed of black robe witches,
And potions,
Sprinkles your mind.

And a dazzling wolf,
Cooks up a soup bowl of deception,
Yellow beads on your heart,
Yellow scars.

Yellow jaded war songs,
Swell your throat.
And then I look below.
I am feeling you.
You live in the mirror.

I live in the world.
Go, go.
I don't need you.
Little Red Riding Hood.

Trajectories of the sky,
And Greek alphabets.
A beautiful life.

I give you mean looks.
You give me blue bells,
Nobody lifts an axe.
No father comes to slay the wolf.

While flowers shower a swimming pool of hopes,
And flowers shade flowers,
There is acid painted on your skin.

I can see it, yes.

I give you pencils.
Write your fate,
You give me blue bells,
You die. ■

50 Way, To Go

Is there no way out?
At the same time,
Each year,
The same feeling advents.
Swinging between two poles,
My heart shrinks.
Two cities.
Was Dickens mad?

There is no door,
No prison.
No escape and no order.
No seditious,
Sacrilege.
A Broadway habit,
Maybe.
No tickets sold for my debut.
Poor me.
Pity me.
Take me to Paris.
Is there no way?

Six inch heels,
Six husbands,
Seventeen sons.
Silly me.
What was I thinking?

Just one short of being Snow White,
With Seven Dwarfs.
Envy me.
Mirrors don't lie.
And poisoned apples don't kill,
Pretty heroines.
Will I ever end?

London Queens still rule,
They still marry Royalty,
And romance temptations.
Their scandals,
Our soups.
Will it ever finish?

Ever, ever after.
I say, I am pretty sleepy.
Between a fascinating dream,
And a nasal real voice,
I choose neither.

Dickens was mad.

51 Through Coloured Eyes

But you were rose to my skin,
And my skin was a wafer,
Glided surreptitiously,
Dropped itself in water,
Got wet,
And faded…
The rose sat and waited.
Why,
Isn't there a window now?
I used to touch you.
We used to touch you.
The lotuses floated,
As the water ran,
The waves and ripples,
Were just promises of seas,
But were actually ponds.
But you were rose to my skin.
You came with words,
Opulent words.
Kissed with a sword,
And left red and saffron blotchy imprints,
On my lips…
So tired were they of words,
That they- bowed and hushed.
On my skin,

Blood trickled like it were milk,
You tickled like a rose.
You shined.
Twenty-four spokes rolled.
More lotuses came with Goddesses.
Blessed me.
Touched me.
I want to touch you.
You were rose to my skin.
A rose indeed-
It was only when I frowned,
You smiled with your tongue,
And I was red, so red in your slavery,
That I shut my eyes,
And all the thorns,
Flew away. ■

52 The Sleep of God

God,
Burn me tonight.
Take a hot iron rod,
Stroke my eyes with it,
Let me go mad.
Mad with a dangerous mind.
Wishful thinking.
And dishonourable intentions.

Ignite me,
Ignite me tonight.
Take a wand dipped in ignited coal.
Tap it on my lips.
Drive me wild.
Wild with a not so chaste mind.
And frenzied fantasies.
Alliterations,
And oxymoronic desires.

Bernini will sculpt me,
Through wells of water,
And the original sin,
Let me take a bite God.
Of the apple I should not touch.
Let me make men fall,
Oh God,
Spill water on my tears,

Of joy,
And canoness.

God,
Consider me.
With a bunch of history,
And Moses,
Behind my back,
I was born,
In something called,
Avila,
Sweet Avila,
I ran away from home,
I knew not what was to be coming ahead,
St. Peter's day,
Illness or celibacy.
A girl of seventeen,
I ran away from home.

Angels whisper in my ears,
And I shudder.
God,
Warm me up.
Take a spade of fire,
Aim at my face,
Aim,
And caress me with heat,
I didn't know what was coming,
When we converted.

From the trial to the convent,
Experiences eluded me.
As the clock hands swayed,
In circles,
And paused,
From time to time,
At a time,
Which was my time,
I saw they were translating,
From Julian to Georgian,
They were flipping paper pages,
Missing and evicting time,
Like it was their slave,
A cathedral of miniature paintings,
And gold,
Built with,
Calendars cementing time.

Barbaric accusations flew,
They doubted me from time to time,
Pure blood,
Never quite lost its value.
And I,
I pleaded God,
I begged to be set free.
Nobody came God,
Nothing,
But a Spanish chill.

Yet,
I was the servant of God,
Closing my butterfly eyes,
I fluttered on my eyelashes,
A utopian spirituality.
My trance was my union,
I levitated when I reached for you God,
I almost reached you,
I was the servant of God.
But I was the servant of Love, God.
The four stages of mysticism,
And ecstasy.

Conception of love,
And God,
In my heart.
My heart pierced by an arrow,
A Seraph drew and withdrew,
And so I could,
I could embrace the down trodden,
Fight the dormant,
Sprout the transformation,
With far sighted eyes,
Of devotion to ecstasy,
I could kiss the Angel,
For the rapture of rhythm,
For the starlight,
Of shimmering prayer,
For the prayer,
Of love.

With deep blue ink,
I wrote,
Imprisoning my light eyes,
With a colour so deep,
That it ran in my blood God,
And I smiled and I cried,
And I amalgamated through an umbilical cord,
Not with my mother,
But with you.

A missionary of buds,
I flowered into something little,
And after I saw you walk and exist,
I existed.
I said, let nothing trouble you,
It is love that stays in every one
Let nothing fret you,
All things pass away,
Only you stay God.

God,
Ring a bell,
Ring and echo it,
Let it hum in my ears,
A sweet song of love,
Purity,
And a clear night sky,
Where,
I am the David star of the church,

Glimmering,
Milky,
Untouched by everything,
But love.

So God,
Pay me back,
In honours,
Or names,
Or Portraits,
In gold coins,
Or guillotines.
With quills,
Of demarcated sects,
And methods of supplication,
I confess,
Lord, either let me suffer,
Or let me die.

Eternity,
Is like the Garden of Eden,
But I am cold God.
So cold.
Ignite me,
And burn me God,
My ashes will pacify,
The distress of life,
And the tribulations,
That flow in rivulets,

Of tears,
Pink noses,
Of sorrow,
And anguish so sweet,
That only you can present it God.

But till then,
I learn,
I write,
And in a granary called Avila,
I am born everyday.
In a brewery,
I am crushed like ripe grapes,
And drunk,
In the wines of,
Avila.

But,
They didn't even know when I died.
Was it the 4th or was it the 15th of October??
Was the sun down or shining that day?
Where were you God when I became sixty-seven years old?
Were my wrinkles,
Like ghosts in the pale moonlight?
Or was my smile marred with experience,
No longer so pious,
Did the candlelight not hide what my robes covered?

When I was losing perception,
Of sensibility,
And time,
I besieged you God,
With death at one corner,
And divinity on my head,
I said,
God, let me not be so good for once,
Let me not silently tip toe on afternoon edges,
Of borderline imaginations,
Of the pleasurable solitude,
Of being with you.
God, let the curtain be raised,
Let the play commence,
Let the puppets dance,
Let the mirrors crack,
From one side to another,
Let a cleft of joy pass,
The shadow of my dreams,
God,
Oh God,
Don't you see?
There is a melancholy,
In the ecstasy of St. Theresa. ■

53 Upturned Skins

Seaming,
Paper like sticks,
To love like stones,
Screaming,
Like a thread of bricks,
A bed of bones,
Heavenly bodies,
My god, they live,
There,
Yes there,
A black hole,
With no coal,
Just colour,
A black shiny pallor,
Ravens,
Cat eyed,
Scavengers,
Sucking
And digging,
Holes of revenge.
Non-feudal.
Non-subjugated.
At atom bomb- of soot.
Sudan. ■

54 Can I Sing To You?

A January star misses him.
Somewhere,
Between layers,
Of thick peacock blue clouds,
Some tresses of a milky constellation,
Lift a magic quill,
And trace a goat.

A January star misses him.
A sleeping midday,
Mesmerized by a dazzling midnight,
Croons,
And tries to imitate him.
Unicorns step on the beginning of a new year.
They know not that it is not just a year.
That light-years away,
And years later,
People will remember them,
As symbols of something that he was part of.
That was part of him.

They wear night robes,
Evening red slippers,
And walk without slipping.
Etching in the condensed droplets,
His eternal name.
Astronomy studies him.

He is the Saturn to sound.
And its rings to music.
Black holes can't wrench, infest and rob a heart as sure as he can.
A night is nothing but a promise of self-reflection,
And helium radiations,
Beyond a starlight and a moonlight.
And the night serenades in awe of him.

And nights pass by,
With wishing stars,
And tail ridden comets.
His voice shoots a star.
A map of a silver lining streaks,
And for a second bleaches,
The thick peacock blue clouds.
And somewhere, near the saturnine moons,
A January star misses him.
Who will give it light now?

The hollowness of our saprophytic,
Natal existence,
Suddenly becomes coloured.
Deep navy blue.
And stars illuminate,
With blinding flashlights,
Flooding the hollowness,
With star rays.
Some things are too beautiful to live.
But do they die?

There is silence.
Swift movements.
Suppressed tears.
A lost love.
A heart break.
A star wreck.
A moonfall.
Saturn rings.

Younger blue clouds scatter,
A horoscope he sketched.
Unaware.

Unaware,
The January star,
Misses him.
Some things are hard to forget.
Hard to recover.
Hard to let go.
Some things are too beautiful; to live.
Some things never die.
And some things decorate the sky,
With milky white grains,
And stay there even when the sun hides them.
Some things are celestial fairytales.
Some things always smile.
And some things,
Are Elvis Presley. ■

55 Men On Moon, Women In Stockings

A bedside lamp,
Fell on the floor today.
It flickered a bit,
But then fused.

The floor shook a bit,
Though the impact has almost become a habit now,
Then it became soft,
So that it hurts less.

Soft cushions,
Got emptied of cotton today.
There was nothing cushy,
Nothing light left.
It cried.

The cotton was rubbed today,
Against a blood gushing wound,
Blood was laughing,
It always had the last laugh.

Blood was residing on a patch of skin,
The skin was scratched.
Poor cousins,
Always used for the wrong reasons.

A bit of the skin,
Fell on the floor,
When skin collaborated with skin,
To skin the so-called bonds.

The floor gave a feeble smile to the skin,
As it became deoxygenated,
The smile fell on the floor,
Everything headed, to vacuum.

The lamp tried to light up again,
The cushion stopped crying after a while,
It got rather sick of it,
And blood became sober…

The skin almost got lost,
And was accompanied by his mother and father,
Almost the very next week
He had nothing to complain about now.

The lamp tried to light up.
Blood knocked at the door more frequently,
Everyone became friends,
And the cushion never smiled again. ■

56 Are You...

Dear lust,
Squeezing out inky eyes,
Paper locks fly in a gassy sky,
Are you caged too?

Gas percolates down,
An ice-cold brinjal mind,
Infects and moistens a seepage,
That harbours a second childhood smile.
Are you wet too?

A stem fragments,
The gas makes it droop.
There is fatherly ink in you.
A Freudal catastrophe.
Rain melts your paper lock,
Yet there is no key.
So how can you vacate the vacuum?
Are you suffocating too?

Canine water dabs you in,
And swallows a tiny point somewhere hidden,
Behind all those scars and wraps of flesh,
Bone and blood,

There is sogginess in your dripping arms,
A blur- in the sluggish hutment of fire.
Water is ink today,
And ink tiptoes on the fringe of my lips,
There trickle brinjal words out,
Words that plaster more such locks on my eyes.
Fire burns a bridge,
And water flames the door.
The gas is ice candy.
And it is water,
That wins tonight.
Dear lust,
Are you sleeping too? ■

57 Objection

A naval ring,
Is my prostitute for the night.
Together we jolt,
Away,
From the air,
Sway,
In the air,
Twist,
In out,
In half made circles,
And come to rest at a center.
It has no bottom.

My moment of weakness,
Is your moment of sparkle.
I see in your eyes,
When you look at me,
My naval ring,
And so many such prostitutes.

It's the only time,
You shine.
So I let it be.
I let it be.
And feel the bottom.

My naval ring stings to my skin.
Close.
It hurts a bit.
But I paid the price.
I want to kiss it.
Only it's not possible.

Then I am exhausted.
And bored of a metal hanging from my tummy,
Like I am a cow,
With a bell tied around my neck.
Only the ring is circular.
It never ends.

Nights drag like poison
And it's difficult dragging my heavy feet towards you.
The naval ring is my prostitute,
And you are mine.

But when I look at you,
Look at me,
I see in your crazy eyes,
Desire.
I am pimping my naval ring now.
There are too many prostitutes in the body,
And the mind.
So,
I let it be,
Let it be,
And,
I belly dance. ■

58 Astigmatism

There you are in a sarong,
When within you is a lusting throng,
You are out battling the urchins of the sea,
And it is raining hot droplets of tea,
And then when you come home to me,
You tremble from the Pasodoble reality,
And a raging bull in your heart,
Eve-teases me to keep us apart,
You are charged with a Saturday storm,
Your dad's wife is not your mom.

In a panic attack,
You thicken to an insomniac,
He tells you to help him with the boats,
Oil the axes, and milk the goats,
And when she tells you she loves you like her own,
A hint of pink sweeps across your skin tone,
But then you think of your summer home,
Where I wait for you with bread and scone,
And the not so happy thought,
Knocks you distraught,
You remember where you came from,
Your dad's wife is not your mom.

A dingy faced tavern,
And liquor makes your eyes burn,
There is a piano tune in your eyes,
That a Beethoven kite flies,
And I see pearls erupt out,
Of your eyes in a disillusioned bout,
Of needle apprehensions,
Of wailing questions,
That mix with your eyes and stir,
Thoughts, I refuse to answer.
You play the moon on your skin,
Destroy my sunny song,
Cleft your gentle chin,
And try to find a new mom.

You became the elastic on my wrinkled forehead,
That earlier, only Astrologers read.
And now you are a sticky balm,
Written by pens of fate on my wrinkled palm.
You look at me in disdain,
And try to jump into my mind,
I push your eyes away in pain,
With the new mom, you could not find.

You could have stopped,
Failed and accepted that you had dropped,

A ring stone from your fingers,
In order to spread your hands apart,
And hunt desperately for more singers,
Jiving to your upstart-
Volcanic song,
To, put your arms around a mom.

And around that time,
Had I cried,
Plastic mornings would have acidified,
Melted and died,
But there you were at my bedside,
Pink gurgling candy eyed,
Was it love or was it failure?
When I felt some ice cream within me disappear?
I felt wounds on my lips,
Wounds in my blood,
Creasing brown leaves on my fingertips,
And green rose buds in a brown mud.
I grew old,
The day I caught hold,
Of your puffy arms,
The day you were told,
That- your dad had other charms.

A toddler fancy took the worse of your vise,
Your frowns built me a candle of ice,

Your silliness glaring at my window,
And your toe ribboned with something I don't know.

It was funny trying to paint a dark ashtray wall,
When life was a yin-yang ping-pong ball.
It was funny, and so it remains,
Till this very saturnine day of iron domains,
Shackles in my heart,
Shackles, on my lips.
You are drenched in a Saturday storm.
And there are things that must depart.
Things; dying on my fingertips.
Things that things have come from.
Things; that are not your mom. ■

59 Shoulders

She comes to me
With a pink painted smile,
Synthesized by toil-
I nod,
Lower my eyes,
Her education begins,
Mine ends
With a crackling of the spine,
And a ten kg baggage,
Her smile brings to me.

My daughter doesn't play games.
She sits in a corner
With pages I can read in five minutes,
My daughter often smiles,
A pink emulation of her mother's...
When I try to lift her up,
She frowns,
When I go to tell her
Bedtime stories and fairytales,
I try and put up,
Pieces she puzzles over,
And I end up,
Bent.

He comes to me,
In a suitcase of files,
Texts, assets, signatures,
I nod again,
Like I am married to them too,
They don't light me up,
But they don't dim me either,
He scraps away my say,
He takes away my voice,
I travel like a pendulum
From infinity to desks and chairs,
And then I hang by a fragile
Small brain thread
Of credit,
And just to hold the thread,
I have to carry,
That baggage from all over;
If I let go of either,
I lose both.
Both;
Forty years of uselessness,
And those two
Facsimile pink plastered
Useless-unhappy smiles. ■

60 Disco-Light Infatuations

Every John Lennon dies.
Chins of knowledge shrink,
Fuzzy rugs and blankets cover the moon,
People stamp weightless feet on moonlit streets,
Streetlamps burn the midnight oil on our digital lips,
And we wander with crimson charcoal wits,
Our hot pancake hearts?
A valentine joke, given to our spouses,
So what have you?

Rhombic radios play derailed old tunes,
You sing in a scoop of noise,
And trend.
I love you,
You love me.
It's the most overexploited emotion,
And yet, it never quite fills up the wine glass,
Liquor splashes on our hearts,
We mark signature dreams,
And autograph promises
On tabloids of steamy coffees,
Gossiping limousines,
And glittering,
Electronic-dance floors.
But then a hand slips under our clothes,
And another moisturizes,

So much so,
That anything that touches it slips through the fingers.
Some people never exchange rings.

We are a singing dancing fumbling phenomenon,
Vampire obsessed,
We contrive ghosts in Italy.
There are too many white rooms,
Full of champagne lights,
Sparkling, just for our fantasy.
We embrace, to engulf all that lies below,
And honey, it's philanthropy.
And honey, it's adoption.
But we keep swaying to a rhythm,
So loud,
That dimmed are old country lyrics,
And old country guitar- parents,
Who lost out a son to the war,
And another to cancer.

Someone ingests a stifling seducing moon,
And manifests immortal nectars on forested bedlams,
Of dreams, illusions and hypotheses.
Someone radiates Cynthia.
And quenches the animal quest for aesthetics,
In an ocean of about-to-be capital mermaids,
And drowns worse than Leonardo DiCaprio,
In an overwhelmingly bright icecap,
Of a totally capital world.

But things of beauty,
Are supposed to last forever,
And what have suppositions come to,
But a discotheque of dance, and more dance.
Keats is an escapist.
Oblivious, to sinusoidal times.
And like the pale brown eyed-poetic Ashley,
Bent to the zest of a Scarlet obsession,
Dies the moment; Melanie passes away;
He dies too,
For those hazel eyes,
Are too soft,
Too estranged, to face a disco-lit spectrum.

Newton faces the spectrum,
Reigns a dry glass slab of academic inventions,
Napoleonalizes a mob of apples,
Dwarf apples,
That fall on the ground,
With silent noises.
But silent noises are no longer in vogue, honey.
And yes, someone surely laments that fall,
For he could have grabbed that ripe red fellow,
And fed some intestine glands,
Neutralized the acidity of science,
With more of those shiny disco balls.
Newton dies too.
When he inverts the magical prism,
He gets white light back.

Some erstwhile English men differ,
Don't like standing in mainstream queues,
Rowing downstream,
Then upstream,
Against the waves.
What kind of a foolish wooden boat,
Is leprechaun enough to battle that out?
They sip their teas,
As if a Soviet prostitute has captivated them.
And she has power enough,
Gorgeous enough,
To keep the boat battling for a while.
On her 29th birthday,
A hint of wrinkles diffuses on her rouge cheekbones,
And then they detest her,
Desert her,
For a cliché of red lipped skimpy blondes.
Marilyn is retarded.
The disco plays more of hip-hopping tunes.
So against what they tried to enforce in the east,
Civilization, and, dilapidation.
Spender is a coward.
His God failed time,
And God failed him.

A bunch of people,
In a bouquet of idiocy,
Hold hands and sit,
With melting wailing, white candles.

They mourn the death of someone,
And assume they are protesting for a while,
While others,
Do the same,
In a dark room,
Away from discoing lights,
Discoing human insights,
To bring back the dead,
Have some impish teenage fun.
Candles are insignificant,
In booming fluorescent disco lights.

Our shoulders droop,
Then swell,
Osmosis has a crush on our eyes,
And onions; on tears.
Songs smile for we glide to their tenors,
Sopranos and operas,
Have class written on their heads with blue inked tattoos.
Taylor swift songs are a joke on Shakespeare,
And Shakespeare; a joke on society.
Words, and quilted words,
Are raindrops now.
Falling flat on a concrete road.
Making a hole,
On a thought-to-be invincible arsenal,
Of sand stone and gypsum glories.
But every John Lennon,

Somehow dies.
Discos become nocturnal facades,
For irradiated realities,
The harshness of stilettos,
And the heat of lip-glosses,
Ignored for the essence,
That comes with dance.
And the darkness,
Emancipated yet illuminated,
By a shiny sexy disco light.

You have a smile.
And a tradition of songs.
And hearts with pre-nuptial desires,
Flower in our cloth prints from time to time.
So what have you?

Sometimes,
I wish I could,
Really could-
Imagine.
But then,
Death takes over the better remains of rationality.
And then,
Rationality seems not too good an excuse.
The discos never halt,
Who wants to die?